187232

PowerKids Readers:

The Bilingual Library of the
United States of America™

MISSOURI
MISURI

JOSÉ MARÍA OBREGÓN

TRADUCCIÓN AL ESPAÑOL: MARÍA CRISTINA BRUSCA

The Rosen Publishing Group's
PowerKids Press™ & **Editorial Buenas Letras**™
New York

Published in 2006 by The Rosen Publishing Group, Inc.
29 East 21st Street, New York, NY 10010

First Edition

Photo Credits: Cover, pp. 23, 31 (Monument) © Richard Cummins/Corbis; p. 5 © Joe Sohm/The Image Works; p. 7 © 2002 Geoatlas; pp. 9, 31 (Spring) © David Muench/Corbis; pp. 11, 19, 25, 30 (Capital), 31 (Twain, Truman, Baker, Parker) © Bettmann/Corbis; pp. 13, 31 (Explorers) © Getty Images; p. 15 © Leonard de Selva/Corbis; pp. 17, 31 (Carver) © Corbis; p. 21 © Aneal Vohra/Index Stock Imagery, Inc.; pp. 26, 30 (Hawthorn) © Mark J. Tweedle, Ecoscene/Corbis; p. 30 (Eastern Bluebird) © Joe McDonald/Corbis; p. 30 (Flowering Dogwood) © Raymond Gehman/Corbis; p. 31 (Blow) Courtesy of Missouri State Archives

Library of Congress Cataloging-in-Publication Data

Obregón, José María, 1963–
Missouri / José María Obregón ; traducción al español, María Cristina Brusca.— 1st ed.
p. cm. — (The bilingual library of the United States of America) Includes bibliographical references and index.
ISBN 1-4042-3090-4 (library binding)
1. Missouri–Juvenile literature. I. Title. II. Series.
F466.3.O23 2006
977.8—dc22
2005010834

Manufactured in the United States of America

Due to the changing nature of Internet links, Editorial Buenas Letras has developed an online list of Web sites related to the subject of this book. This site is updated regularly. Please use this link to access the list:

http://www.buenasletraslinks.com/ls/missouri

Contents

Contenido

Welcome to Missouri

These are the flag and seal of the state of Missouri. The flag was designed and hand sewn by Marie Elizabeth Watkins Oliver and Mary Kochtitzky in 1913.

Bienvenidos a Misuri

Estos son la bandera y el escudo del estado de Misuri. La bandera fue diseñada y cosida a mano en 1913 por Marie Elizabeth Watkins Oliver y Mary Kochtitzky.

Missouri Flag and State Seal

Bandera y escudo de Misuri

Missouri Geography

Missouri borders the states of Iowa, Illinois, Kentucky, Tennessee, Arkansas, Oklahoma, Kansas, and Nebraska. Two important rivers run throughout the state, the Mississippi River and the Missouri River.

Geografía de Misuri

Misuri linda con los estados de Iowa, Kentucky, Tennessee, Arkansas, Oklahoma, Kansas y Nebraska. Dos ríos importantes atraviesan el estado, el río Misisipi y el río Misuri.

IOWA

ILLINOIS

Missouri River
Río Misuri

Missouri River
Río Misuri

Independence

Kansas City

St. Louis
San Luis

KANSAS

Jefferson City

MISSOURI
MISURI

Mississippi River
Río Misisipi

KENTUCKY

Springfield

OKLAHOMA

ARKANSAS

TENNESSEE

Map of Missouri

Mapa de Misuri

Missouri is famous for its many springs. A spring is a place where water rises up from the earth. Big Springs in southeastern Missouri is located on the Ozark National Scenic Riverways. Big Springs is one of the largest springs in the world.

Misuri es famoso por sus manantiales. Un manantial es un lugar en donde el agua brota naturalmente desde abajo de la tierra. El manantial Big Springs está al sureste de Misuri, en el Ozark National Scenic Riverways. Big Springs es uno de los manantiales más grandes del mundo.

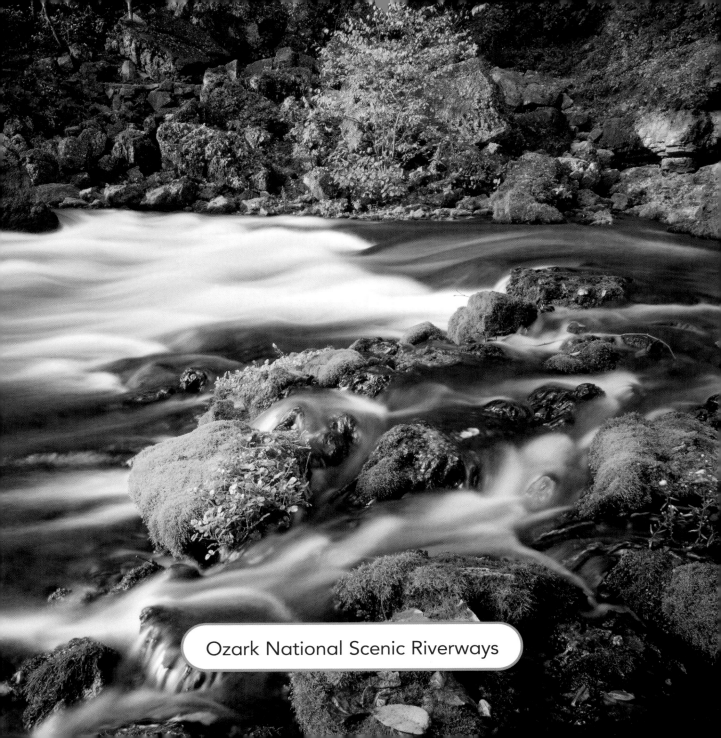

Ozark National Scenic Riverways

Missouri History

In 1673, two French explorers, Father Jacques Marquette and Louis Jolliet became the first Europeans to visit the Missouri area. Since then, France, Spain, and the United States have controlled the state.

Historia de Misuri

En 1673, dos franceses, el Padre Jacques Marquette y Louis Jolliet fueron los primeros europeos en explorar el territorio de Misuri. Desde entonces, Francia, España y los Estados Unidos han controlado el estado.

Marquette and Jolliet Traveling the Mississippi River

Marquette y Jolliet en su viaje por el río Misisipi

In 1805, Meriwether Lewis and William Clark left St. Louis, Missouri, for an important trip. Lewis and Clark were looking for a route to the Pacific Ocean. This trip opened the western territories to the United States.

En 1805, Meriwether Lewis y William Clark partieron de St. Louis, Misuri, en un viaje muy importante. Lewis y Clark estaban buscando una ruta al océano pacífico. Este viaje abrió para los Estados Unidos los territorios del oeste.

Meriwether Lewis and William Clark

Meriwether Lewis y William Clark

The Pony Express started in Saint Joseph, Missouri, in 1860. Men on horses carried mail from Saint Joseph to Sacramento, California. This trip is almost 2,000 miles (3,219 km) long. It took 10 days to deliver a letter.

En 1860, se inauguró en Misuri un sistema de correo llamado Pony Express. Jinetes a caballo llevaban cartas desde Saint Joseph hasta Sacramento, California. Era un viaje de casi 2,000 millas (3,219 km). Se tardaba 10 días para entregar una carta.

ST. JOSEPH

UNITED STATES POSTAGE

SACRAMENTO

4c

1860·1960 PONY EXPRESS

This Postal Stamp Honors the Pony Express

Esta estampilla honra el Pony Express

St. Louis, Missouri, was the home of the World's Fair in 1904. A world's fair showed inventions from around the world. The first hot dogs and ice-cream cones were shown in the St. Louis World's Fair.

San Luis, Misuri, fue la sede de la Exposición Mundial de 1904. En una exposición mundial se muestran inventos de todas partes del mundo. En la Exposición Mundial de San Luis se dieron a conocer los conos de helado y los perritos calientes o *hot dogs*.

The 1904 World's Fair in St. Louis

La Exposición Mundial de San Luis de 1904

Samuel Clemens was born in Missouri in 1835. He was a writer who changed his name to Mark Twain. He wrote books about growing up on the Mississippi River. Twain wrote *The Adventures of Tom Sawyer* and *The Adventures of Huckleberry Finn.*

Samuel Clemens nació en Misuri en 1835. Clemens fue un escritor que cambió su nombre a Mark Twain y escribió libros acerca de la vida de los jóvenes en el río Misisipi. Twain escribió *Las aventuras de Tom Sawyer* y *Las aventuras de Huckleberry Finn.*

Samuel Clemens (Mark Twain) in 1903

Samuel Clemens (Mark Twain) en 1903

Living in Missouri

Kansas City, Missouri, calls itself the Barbecue Capital of the World. The American Royal Barbecue is the largest barbecue contest in the world. Thousands of Missourians visit the contest every year.

La vida en Misuri

Kansas City, Misuri se llama a sí misma La Capital Mundial de la Barbacoa. La *American Royal Barbecue* es el concurso de este tipo más grande del mundo. Cada año, miles de misurianos visitan esta competencia.

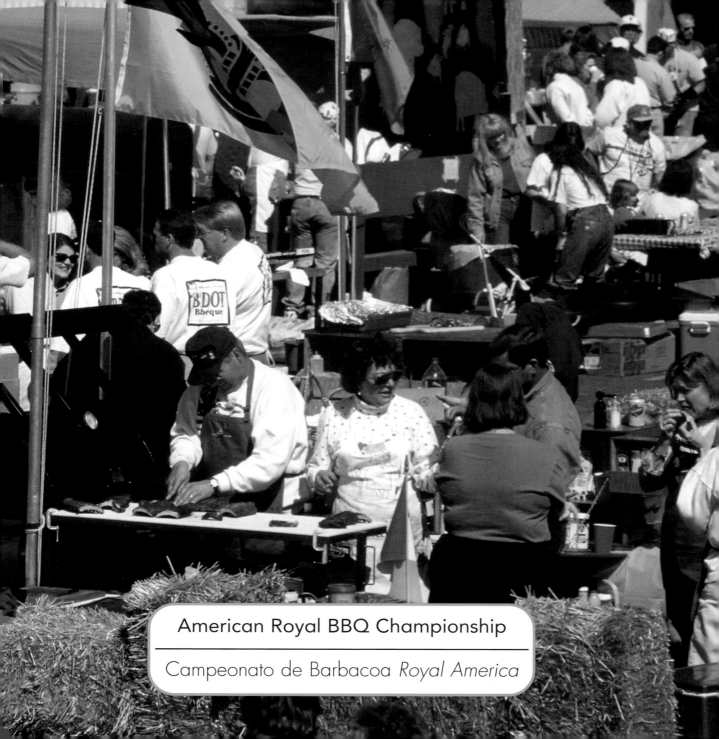

American Royal BBQ Championship

Campeonato de Barbacoa *Royal America*

Missouri is called the Gateway to the West. The state is considered a midpoint between the eastern and the western United States. St. Louis, Missouri, marks this with the Gateway Arch, a 630-foot-(192 m) high monument.

Misuri es conocida como la Entrada al Oeste. Misuri está ubicado en el centro de los Estados Unidos, entre los estados del este y los del oeste. San Luis, Misuri celebra esto con un monumento de 630 pies (192 m) de altura llamado Arco de Entrada.

The Gateway Arch

El Arco de Entrada

Kansas City, St. Louis, Springfield, and Independence are important cities in Missouri. Jefferson City is the capital of the state.

Kansas City, San Luis, Independence y Springfield son ciudades importantes de Misuri. Jefferson City es la capital del estado.

Missouri State Capitol in Jefferson City

Capitolio del estado de Misuri en Jefferson City

Activity:
Let's Draw Missouri's State Flower

The hawthorn became Missouri's state flower in 1923.

Actividad:
Dibujemos la flor del estado de Misuri

El espino blanco es la flor del estado de Misuri desde 1923

1

Draw a small circle inside a larger circle.

Dibuja un pequeño círculo adentro de un círculo mayor.

2

Add five large ovals for petals.

Agrega cinco óvalos grandes en el lugar de los pétalos.

3

Use curved lines to connect the petals to the smaller circle. Shape the outer edges of the petals with pointed curved lines.

Usa líneas curvas para conectar los pétalos al círculo pequeño. Dale forma al borde de los pétalos con líneas curvas que terminen en punta. Borra las líneas innecesarias.

4

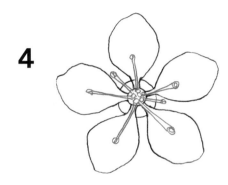

Erase extra lines. Draw tiny circles inside the flower's smallest circle. Draw long, thin shapes from the tiny circles you just drew. Add small, round shapes at the end.

Dibuja círculos muy pequeñitos adentro del círculo pequeño. Partiendo de los círculos pequeñitos que recién has dibujado, traza formas estrechas y alargadas. Agrégales unas formas redondas en el extremo.

5

Add shading. Great job!

Agrega sombras. ¡Buen trabajo!

Timeline

Cronología

Sieur de La Salle travels down the Mississippi and claims the land for France.	**1682**	Sieur de La Salle viaja por el río Misisipi y reclama la tierra para Francia.
St. Louis is founded by Pierre Laclède.	**1784**	Pie Laclède funda San Louis.
The Louisiana Purchase gives the U.S. control over the Mississippi River.	**1803**	La Compra de Luisiana le da a los Estados Unidos el control del río Misisipi.
The strongest earthquake in U.S. history shakes the area near New Madrid.	**1811**	El mayor terremoto de la historia de los E.U.A. sacude la zona cercana a New Madrid.
Missouri becomes the twenty-fourth state.	**1821**	Misuri se convierte en el estado veinticuatro.
The First Olympic games in the United States take place in St. Louis. St. Louis hosts the World's Fair.	**1904**	Las Olimpíadas tienen lugar, por primera vez en los E.U.A., en San Luis. San Luis es la sede de la Exposición Mundial.
The "flood of the century" causes great damage in Missouri.	**1993**	La "inundación del siglo" causa grandes daños en Misuri.
Missouri governor Mel Carnahan dies in a plane crash.	**2000**	El gobernador de Misuri, Mel Carnahan, muere en un accidente de aviación.

Missouri Events | Eventos en Misuri

Missouri Events	Eventos en Misuri
March State trout season opening in Montauk State Park	Marzo Inauguración de la temporada estatal de la trucha, en el Parque Estatal Mountake
April Pony Express celebration in St. Joseph Turkey-calling championships in Kirksville	Abril Celebraciones del Pony Express, en St. Joseph Campeonato de llamadores de pavo, en Kirksville
May Storytelling Festival in St. Louis	Mayo Festival de narradores, en San Luis
June Riverfest at Cape Girardeau	Junio Fiesta del río, en Cabo Girardeau
July National Tom Sawyer Days in Hannibal Fair St. Louis	Julio Día nacional de Tom Sawyer, en Hannibal Feria de San Luis
September Annual American Royal Barbecue in Kansas City	Septiembre Barbacoa Anual Real Americana, en Kansas City
November-December Ozark Mountain Christmas near Branson	Noviembre-Diciembre Navidad en las Montañas Ozark, alrededores de Branson

Missouri Facts/Datos sobre Misuri

<u>Population</u>
5.5 million

<u>Población</u>
5.5 millones

<u>Capital</u>
Jefferson City

<u>Capital</u>
Jefferson City

<u>State Motto</u>
The Welfare of the
People Shall Be the
Supreme Law

<u>Lema del estado</u>
El bienestar del pueblo
debe ser la ley
suprema

<u>State Flower</u>
Hawthorn

<u>Flor del estado</u>
Espino blanco

<u>State Bird</u>
Eastern Bluebird

<u>Ave del estado</u>
Azulejo oriental

<u>State Nickname</u>
The Show Me State

<u>Mote del estado</u>
Ver para creer

<u>State Tree</u>
Flowering dogwood

<u>Árbol del estado</u>
Cornejo en flor

<u>State Song</u>
"The Missouri Waltz"

<u>Canción del estado</u>
"El vals de Misuri"

Famous Missourians/Misurianos famosos

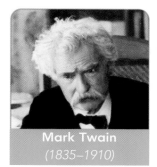

Mark Twain
(1835–1910)

Author
Escritor

Susan Elizabeth Blow
(1843–1916)

Educator
Educadora

George Washington Carver *(1864–1943)*

Scientist
Científico

Harry S. Truman
(1884–1972)

U.S. President
Presidente de los E.U.A.

Josephine Baker
(1906–1975)

Dancer
Bailarina

Charlie Parker
(1920–1955)

Jazz saxophonist
Saxofonista de jazz

Words to Know/Palabras que debes saber

border
frontera

explorers
exploradores

monument
monumento

spring
manantial

Here are more books to read about Missouri:
Otros libros que puedes leer sobre Misuri:

In English/En inglés:

Missouri
From Sea to Shining Sea
by Lago, Mary Ellen
Children's Press, 2003

Missouri
This Land Is Your Land
by Heinrichs, Ann
Compass Point Books, 2003

Words in English: 373

Palabras en español: 409

Index

Índice